Men Without Hats
Shaun Payne

-Payneful Publishing-

Copyright 2022 Shaun Payne

All rights reserved. No part of this publication may be reproduced, stored in a retrieval system or transmitted in any form, or by any means (electronic, mechanical, photocopying, recording or otherwise), without the prior permission of the publisher. Any person who does so may be liable to criminal prosecution and civil claims for damages.

The right of Shaun Payne to be identified as author of this work has been asserted.

First published in 2022 by Payneful Publishing.

This edition printed by 4edge Ltd

ISBN 978-1-3999-3577-7

This book is sold subject to the condition that it shall not be lent, resold, hired out or otherwise circulated without the publisher's express prior consent in any form of binding or cover, other than the original as herein published and without a similar condition being imposed on any subsequent purchaser or bona fide possessor.

This is a work of fiction, and all characters are drawn from the author's imagination. Any resemblances to persons either living or dead are entirely coincidental. Believe that and you'll believe anything.

Dedicated to my darlin' daughter, Jade Taylor.
Sorry for the inherited unsettled gene.

Many thanks to my old friend, Geoff Tristram, without whose contribution, this book would never have seen the light of day, so blame him.

Also, to his better half, Susan, for endless cups of tea.

Contact the author at:
shaunpayne1955@yahoo.com

Chapter 1

What a weird dream. I didn't exactly bounce out of my bed, full of the joys of spring – well, I wouldn't would I, it being a typical English November Monday morning. Looking out of my window, it's dark, damp, dismal, and drizzly. Here we go, shut up. I'm not going to say depressing; I'm pink and breathing – always a good sign. I tuck into my regular breakfast, coffee, porridge, chopped-up banana with a drizzle of honey over the top. Then I'm ready to face the world – I think. I need to fill up on supplies. Always leave it till I'm down to my last egg, and I'm scraping the last drop of honey from the jar. That's because I don't venture out much. I'm quite content with my own company, in my little cocoon, and letting the world get on with whatever it's doing. I like what I'm doing, which could be described by some as nothing. Who can say? Nothing, something, anything, one can be positive or negative about any of these terms. Does it really matter what anyone thinks? Whose opinion counts anyway? We're all fed the same bullshit on a daily basis. TV, newspapers, politics – voters never learn. I think it was a quote coined by Mark Twain.

"If voting made a difference, it wouldn't be allowed."

It's all rigged, *everything!* Some vote for the crap they swallow, either that, or they take a personal shine to the slickest candidate, who promises to deliver the goods, and never does, and then the speech is shredded, pulped, recycled, and made into more paper for the next manifesto. And round and round it goes. I'm a cynical bugger, but I am a happy cynical bugger. Before I go out any morning, I play a little harmonica, just to get on the neighbour's tits, ha ha! And a little writing. Songs and tunes, little ditties, just for my own entertainment. I'm easily entertained. Okay, coat on, list, money, out I go into a blustery day. Head down, I'm just about to enter the store. A voice from behind shouts,

"Hey you!"

I turn around to be confronted by a big, intimidating hairy-faced guy. "Me?"

"Yes," he bawls, "I don't see anyone else here, do you?"

"Er, no," I say,

"Where's your hat," he says.

"Hat?"

"Yes, your hat!"

"What hat?"

"*Your* hat, moron.'

"I don't have a hat."

"You don't have a hat? What are you, stupid? You been living under a rock? Now, last time, where is your hat?"

"This is some kind of joke, right?"

"You see me laughing?" he asks.

"I don't *have* a hat. Why do I need a hat," I reply.

At that, he blows a whistle. Two big guys pounce from a nearby vehicle, grab my wrists, pushing them hard up the centre of my back, and frogmarch me to a nearby black van.

"Phone?" growls one heavy.

"Yes, my right-hand pocket."

He rifles through my jacket, takes my phone and adds it to a dozen or so more in a metal box, and then I'm thrown unceremoniously into and amongst maybe ten or twelve fearful looking faces, and the door slams shut.

"What the hell is going on?" I scream, to a bunch of guys with their heads down.

"Sshh. Don't say nothing," says a voice in the dark.

"What! Am I missing something here?"

"A hat, obviously," came a wry reply.

"Is this a joke? This is a put-up, yeah, or what?"

"Didn't you hear, read or see on TV, hats for men are compulsory."

"It's the law now," says another.

"Since when?" I ask.

"Since last week, apparently," another guy explains.

"A man's head cannot be seen without a hat in a public place."

"Are you serious? Where to now?"

"Who knows."

"And why a God-damn hat?" someone mutters.

"A hat is your identification, it defines who and what you are; your religion, your club, your status, everything."

"Where are we going?" I ask my fellow travellers.

"We don't know – no idea."

"Do you see any windows in this tin can?"

"Maybe we'll stop at a bar, shoot some pool, catch a movie on the way back to wherever. Mmm!" comments one smart-arse.

"Just shut the hell up, will ya!" shouts another.

Half an hour or so we slow down to the sound of a grinding roller shutter door.

"Now what?"

We stop, eye-whites are rolling around through the dim light. Doors of the van open.

"Okay, out, orderly line," a gruff voice instructs us.

"Say nothing, not a whisper, got it!" he shouts.

We step tentatively out of the van to the sight of a large courtyard. Grey stone walls towering some thirty feet high surrounding us, and two blinding arc lights scrutinising our screwed-up expressions. We look at one-another in bewilderment, and begin to give our captors our names, addresses and dates of birth. Any forms of I.D. we possess are confiscated and put into a file.

"Okay," says a uniformed official. "Follow me, eyes forward."

We walk through a dimly-lit archway and carefully negotiate a flight of steps; forty or more descending underground. Moans and groans become audible. We begin to slow down to a crawl, fearing what might await us; and are abruptly ordered to get a move on.

"Come on, move it." I'm given a push along.

Bundled into what resembles a wartime bunker, we turn into a long dull, damp concrete passageway. Signs indicating numbered holding cells. A guard at each heavy door, jangling keys, smiling as if we're being welcomed to the Bangkok Hilton.

"Christ's sake!" someone in front of me cries, followed by a hard smack on the back of his head, dispensed by our host.

"Shut up!" he commands.

"Okay, here, five to a cell. Make yourselves at home."

No seating, no beds, just a cold concrete floor. A shithole in the corner. A blanket and a bottle of water each.

"Now, listen up," says our host, "you paying attention?"

"You will be monitored. Everything you say and discuss will be heard and could determine the time you remain here; and may also reveal *what* you are – or not."

The door is banged shut and locked. No more information on why we are here, apart from our lack of a hat. Or what process we are to go through, nothing, and what about the last words uttered by the guard?

"May also reveal *what* you are – or not."

What the hell could that mean? What a weird statement. Everyone's stumm, afraid to say anything for fear of being labelled spokesman for the group, I guess.

Chapter 2

Morning comes after a very long night of trying to get some measure of comfort. Daylight struggles to appear through an unreachable tiny window. Bodies begin to move like cripples, all stiff as boards, trying to get in the best possible position on a rock-hard floor throughout the night. I had ten or twenty minutes of shut-eye, I think, trying to absorb this situation. What about my folks? What are they thinking? Have they been informed? Are they visiting every hospital; every morgue to know my whereabouts? Christ, I'll bet they've had less sleep than me. *I don't think.*

Time is dragging to a standstill now. When is that door gonna clank open? They do what they're gonna do and send us on our merry way for, for Christ's sake.

"Anybody got any ideas on this?" I say.

There's silence, and crumpled faces stare back at me.

"Anybody?"

"Say something, anything."

"You're the only one rattling on, pal," said the guy who received the smack on the back of his head.

"I nominate you, the brains of the outfit."

"Okay, okay. Guess we're all in the shit, right?

At that, the sound of movement further on down the passageway, keys jangling, locks being turned, heavy metal doors screeching open. Mumbles and grumbles, ordered to shut up.

Another hour or so later, our door unlocks and opens to reveal two burly guys. The five of us struggle to our feet. They greet us with a grunt, one holding a clipboard.

"Name, just your names."

"Shane Paine," I say.

"Next!"

"Okay, get in line."

"You lot, you're next up before the beak. 15 minutes."

What, me before the beak, like I'd committed a serious crime in my sleep I was unaware of?

Up the steps we go, catching our first glimpse of daylight in twenty-four hours. Everyone looks like shit, so I guess I look the same. Smell like it too. I alone proceed to be escorted by my two pug-like chaperones into a packed courtroom, everyone in the gallery wearing a different bloody hat. Sneering upon my entrance in disapproval of my dishevelled appearance, and I guess my lack of a hat.

"Silence," howls the clerk.

In walks the beak, wig and all.

"Be seated. Defendant, rise."

That's me, by all accounts!

"Champagne!" he bellows.

Uh, methinks it's a party. He's ordered champagne, it's all a big prank, a joke. Did I wake up?

"Champagne!" he bellows again.

"Huh! he's addressing me. "No, sir, *Shane* Paine, sir," I proclaim.

"Mmm," he sighs.

Then authoritatively demands, "What are you?"

"What *am* I?" I reply."

"Mr Paine, I ask the questions in this courtroom. Do you have the intellect to answer them? Or do you require counsel?" His voice raised with contempt. "This court will not endure impertinence. Do you understand?"

"Yes, sir, but!"

"But nothing. Answer the question put to you, very simply, what are you?"

"Sir, I'm not quite sure what you mean. I'm going about my business, when I'm picked up, for not wearing a hat."

"EXACTLY!" he cries, his voice losing patience.

"Mr Paine, look around this courtroom. Do you see anyone *not* wearing a hat?"

"No, sir."

"No, sir, indeed," he retorts.

"Mr Paine, look again around this courtroom. Do you observe in the gallery there are soldiers, sailors, Sikhs, Jews, Muslims, a whirling dervish hat, and a Ku Klux Klan hat, amongst others, all wearing the appropriate attire, and all law-abiding citizens. Mr Paine, do you understand the gravity of the offence for not wearing a hat, and not declaring what you are, for the wellbeing of society?"

"No, sir," I mutter.

"Then I will inform you," he says. "If you cannot proclaim what you are by means of a hat, you will spend not more than three months on the offshore colony for 'Men Without Hats.' In that given time, you will possibly reflect and presumably decide what you are. After you receive counselling and training. However, you have twenty-four hours before you reappear in this courtroom for the final verdict on your immediate future. Do you understand?"

"I think so, sir."

"Then think hard, Mr Paine. Hopefully for your sake, you will have come to your senses before tomorrow's appearance, avoid the colony, and resume your life as before, but with a more purposeful existence. Take him down."

Up until now, this was all so surreal, like I'd been whisked into another mad world, and I was going to wake up any minute now. But as I staggered out of the courtroom, reality hit me like a huge slap in the face. Was this for real? Real as it gets, it seems.

"Where's my phone?" I demanded. "I want my phone. I need to inform my people, let them know what's happening."

"No phones," came a stern reply from my escort.

"Well, when, when?"

"When you have decided *what* you are," he says.

Delivered back to my cell, I sit down, back against the wall, head in my hands, not looking at or acknowledging any of my cell mates, just thinking so hard. It's impossible to focus on any one thought. I need to calm down. Twenty-four hours to decide what I am.

Chapter 3

What am I? What do I say I am, to get the hell out of this joint? It's going to be bullshit anyway, whatever I say, and they will see right through it. I'm an atheist. I don't belong to any group or political party. I have no particular interests or prejudices. I don't belong to any club. Hell, I wouldn't even join a Christmas Club. My mind is racing now, going nowhere fast. I must have just fallen asleep through sheer mental exhaustion when I am awoken by the opening of the cell door, each of us presented with a tray of slop of some sorts. A harmless plastic spoon and a bottle of water. How tasty and welcome shit food is when you haven't eaten for more than a day. Michelin star? Not quite, but edible, just.

Once eaten, I'd just begun to nod off again when the guy next to me gives me a nudge and says, "wonder what's for pudding?".

I could have smacked him square in the face, until the others raised a little chortle. So, I managed a wry smile, and we all began a whispered group conversation, well aware we were being observed and listened to.

For the next hour or so we were exchanging banter.

"I'm going to say I'm a king," said one crazy half-wit, and was told by another of similar ilk, "That's stupid, you'll be locked up forever, and just imagine if they were to believe you, and say, okay, 'Your Royal Highness', put a crown on your head, and stuff you in a gilded cage, isolated, only let out on special ceremonial occasions, to cruise around in a golden, horse-drawn carriage, waving at every common twat."

"No, no. You'd be better off saying you're a peasant. You'd be unkempt, in tatters, wearing a greasy leather skull-cap, eating gruel and turnips, tugging your forelock at everyone you encounter, but you'd be as free as a bird, see?"

I'm looking on in disbelief, as these two are actually contemplating these options. I'm in a madhouse.

"No, no," pipes up someone else, making me wish I was deaf.

I can't listen to this crap. Eyes are great; you can just close them. I can't think now. We're all cramped up here together but we're all alone. Now think, think, think, asshole. What do I do? What do I say I am? What am I? The pressure's mounting. Right now, I would join a Christmas Club, just to get a stupid hat, a hat with reindeer horns covered in bloody tinsel, handing out crap in the local mall to spoilt rugrats once a year, if it got me outa this jam. Christ's sake! That's it, that's it, ain't it funny how Christ or God always comes into it when shit hits the fan. Churchill or someone said there were no atheists in the trenches. Okay, I'm unemployed, can't wear a carpenter's hat, a tiler's hat or a decorator's hat. Dunno if they'd count anyway, but I could volunteer for the Salvation Army. Mmm. Or, or enlist in the regular army. No, don't be stupid, I couldn't shoot some bugger. Or maybe I could if he was taking pot shots at me. But I'm too old now anyways.

Mind's working overtime now and time's slipping away. I either get out of here tomorrow morning or spend the next three months on an island with a bunch of morons shooting the shit, day and night. That's not fair. Out of five guys, including myself, I've only observed two morons, three out of five ain't bad, assuming my self-analysis as a non-moron isn't self-delusional. A quote come to mind, looking at this pair, still considering the 'prince and the pauper' logic. 'Ignorance is bliss'. They can't be aware that they're morons. Stop it! What am I thinking? Focus asshole, time's running out. I need to shut down for an hour. Bloody hell, it stinks in here. I can feel the slop going right through me. There's no way I can take a dump in front of everyone. Can't do that! I hope maybe I can last till the morning – or not; there's a little rumbling going on, oh no! Anyway, plan B, Salvation Army, that's what I'll say I am! They're gonna say, where's the hat? Lost it! Did you report it lost? Er, left it at home. What's your address? We'll go pick it up. How long have you been in the Salvation Army? Er, I can feel myself digging a big hole here; I'm just going to bury myself in it. Hardly know much of anything from the Bible anyway; never one for fairy stories or doctrines to control the masses. Water into wine though, that's a nice parable. Yeah, now I'm getting ridiculous. The colony offshore, maybe it's a nice island, white sandy beaches, palm trees, nice hotel, small stroll away and three-square meals a day, come on, get a grip. Nobody would wear a stupid hat.

Chapter 4

Phew! Hot and sticky in here now. I wonder what my compatriots are going to declare. Not much hope for two of them, I can guess. Not much hope for me either, unless I get my head together and come up with a plan.

Six or so hours to go, I'm guessing, seeing as no one has a watch. Just relying on the faint sign of daylight appearing through the small window. Is it too late for me to tell the beak I am 'willing' to join a group, any club, any religion. It could be construed as a desperate attempt to save my ass, risking the book being thrown at me, but it's gotta be worth a try, as a last resort.

I need to compose myself. Look sincere, straight-backed when I face that asshole who decides whether I walk or not. Sounds final. Come on, there has to be a simple way out of this. I'm not a bad guy. I've never made unwilling little old ladies cross a busy street, never kicked a dog, and never, ever, blown up a frog with a straw up its ass. What have I done so wrong? I've no previous criminal convictions, only one misdemeanour when I was thirteen years old.

I, along with another kid, broke into a Scout hut and stole a pair of deer antlers and various other horned trophies from the walls, to display in my bedroom. I got arrested on a return visit, attempting to take more, and, of course, the police came to my house looking for more loot. Made a list, deer antlers, buffalo horns, etc., and told my folks to return them to the Police Station as soon as possible. My brother, who was around twelve months old at the time, was transported around in an old-fashioned high pram, the only form of wheeled transport in my family, apart from my sister's roller skates.

So, next day, four mounted horn trophies were carefully placed in the pram on top of my screaming baby brother, along with our unruly German shepherd, 'Rusty', tied by his lead to the handle of the pram, and off we headed to the local cop shop. What a picture my mother's face was, red with embarrassment and rage as we walked through the local shopping centre of the High Street, looking down on me with gritted teeth.

"In no uncertain terms," she whispered, "if you ever do anything like this again, I will kill you." I believed her.

People out shopping were gawping and quite amused, and I'm sure I lip-read 'Rosemary's baby', a couple of times. I can laugh about it now, but at the time it was awful. Anyway, surely that's not still on record from fifty years ago, cannot be. I received a five-pound fine and for two hours every Saturday for six weeks, I had to march around a school playground, screwing up the best day of the week of my school holidays.

Chapter 5

A hat, a hat, my kingdom for a hat. I'm sure there's a book entitled: 'The Ramblings of a Madman'. I'm beginning to think it was written for me. Right now, we're all looking at each other disdainfully and defeated, as if we're headed for the gallows. Apart from the two morons who think all this is some kinda game, and the best outcome for them would be going on a cruise to an island and being fed and watered for the next three months; probably a great improvement on their shit life, if their appearance is anything to go by.

Wonder what my folks are thinking? Do they know I'm here? Has there been a report of my arrest? Thing is, I never heard, not even a whisper, about this law being proposed, never mind passed. That's because I don't read newspapers or watch TV., newspapers, apart from the puzzles and crosswords, are only fit for wiping your ass. They really should soften up that paper and maybe make it two-ply. And the last time I watched TV for all of ten minutes, I wanted to put my boot through the screen. But it so happens, it was my Ma's TV.

I've heard people say, newspapers are a waste of paper, TV. is a load of dross, but they still read pulp and tune in like addicts. And there they go, every morning, strolling to the local newsagent, walking back home with a newspaper rolled up under their arm, to sit and read the same old crap with a cup of Rosie Lea. Then, like clockwork, morning TVs turned on to the drone of 'Lorraine bloody Kelly', and that repulsive dishwater duo, Phil and Holly. How do supposedly normal people get immersed in that bilge and continue watching the dumbing down of the nation?

Same as the music scene. Whatever happened to the music revolution anyway? The 50s was when the world changed from 'How Much is That Doggy in the Window?' to 'The Jailhouse Rock', progressing through the 60s, the 70s, then, come the 80s, post-punk rock, everything spiralled down the pan. It all got sickly sweet, the New Romantics, glossy videos, manufactured boy and girl bands who wouldn't have a clue how to ring a bell. No musical abilities, just a shower of pouters prancing around to a synthesised beat, nothing original to get you thinking, only bleeding hearts, guys singing like little girls getting their hair pulled. Sam Smith, whining away relentlessly, Bruno Mars, proclaiming that he'd take a bullet for his girlfriend, or boyfriend, *I don't know*, but I wish he'd hurry up about it. A few good bands got through the cracks though, and there's still some great stuff coming out, but mainstream? Pass me the bucket?

Now I'm ranting instead of thinking about the real issue at hand. 'What am I?' The more times I say that to myself, the less I understand it, and the more cryptic it becomes. Maybe I need to spend three months on the colony, make me more humbling, less cynical and critical, or would it?

I could be a more compassionate person towards my fellow man. Who knows, I might just find my calling. They can't all be moronic there. There may just be some real intellectuals amongst them who maybe refuse to wear a hat on the grounds of discrimination. We can't all be pigeonholed and recognised for one particular interest or affiliation.

I'm not the Brain of Britain, I know, so maybe I could learn something. Would anyone who flatly refused to wear a hat and toe the line ever be allowed to leave the colony though, for fear of subversive behaviour, once repatriated amongst the general population? Less than likely.

I think it's best, come the worst scenario, I keep myself to myself, and not get tarred with anyone's brush. No, I've got to get the hell out of here by hook or by crook. Who knows what goes on in that place. Could be a facility for social, medical experiments, brainwashing. We could all end up as lab rats for new drugs. I'm beginning to feel defeated. I'm not coming up with anything remotely original that's going to get me out of this fix, and that's not like me. In the past, I've managed to get myself out of some pretty precarious predicaments, scrapes and awkward situations.

One time, for instance, many years ago, I had a contract to fix up a themed pub-cum-restaurant just outside Glasgow. I'd never been to Scotland before. I was introduced to Terry by the boss of the company supplying all the fixtures and fittings. Terry was an ex-marine, not very tall, but built like a brick shithouse. He was to be my work partner on this job for around the next three weeks. Very handy guy, I was told.

Anyway, after what seemed an endless drive, we arrived in bonnie Scotland, found the pub-restaurant easily, big place. Giant rolls of carpet had just been delivered and foam for the seating that we had to make; looked pretty comfy. So, we decided the cash we'd been given for digs would stay in our arse pockets, and we'd bed down here for the duration. It was a massive place, plenty of room to run around, just ourselves. But within three days of just work and no play, and not straying from the complex, cabin fever began to set in. We were both gagging for a beer.

So, come around 7.00pm, we went walkabout, passing pub after pub, knowing full well the English were not that popular north of the border. We gave the rowdy establishments a wide berth, and came to a kinda social club, women, children, safe environment. Some kind of Bank Holiday, dunno what. But guys in kilts, blades tucked down the sides of high socks doing the highland fling, I guess. Cautiously, we walked through the room. I asked what looked like an extended family would they mind if we joined their twenty-seater table.

"No, sit doon!" said one old grandma.

Great. We're drinking away, three, four, five pints later, feeling well-oiled, when grandma next to me shouts out of the blue, "Are you protty or cathy?".

I instantly felt my guts roll 360 degrees. I knew what she meant, but I played dumb.

"Sorry, what?" I said.

And she repeated and elaborated a few decibels louder.

"Are you PROTESTANT or CATHOLIC?"

And in a fraction of a second, I quipped, "Oh, I don't know, I never had religion. I was brought up in a children's home." And miraculously, I was instantly dismissed. Phew! Was that a good God-damn answer or what! But then my buddy, Terry, who'd been listening in, pipes up and stupidly retorted,

"What difference does it make anyway."

Dope! why did he have to stoke a potential fire.

At that, a guy opposite stands up, six-foot-four at least, in skinhead attire, covered in home-done tattoos, most notably a swastika in the centre of his forehead, and shouts,

"It makes a lot of fuckin' difference around here, pal."

Oh God! we're dead meat, oh no, oh no.

And then another miracle. Some national tune starts blasting out the speakers. The whole place erupted, and everyone made a scramble to the dance floor. In the confusion, I thumbed to Terry, let's get the hell out of here. We made a beeline to the exit and raced outa the door like greyhounds leaving the traps. Shit, lucky or what!

Chapter 6

If only I could come up with the same convincing bullshit to put before the beak later today, he may also dismiss me – that would be another miracle.

Come on, please, please, think, scatterbrain. Instead of going off on a tangent every ten minutes. How long now? We've eaten our slop. Can't be that long. I try to engage in conversation with the other two guys that I've prematurely presumed 'normal', but they're offish, obviously working on their own defensive stories. So, I get back into my little shell.

I'm thinking to myself, it looks very much like I'm going on a boat trip. At that, one of the morons begins to sing, 'Oh, a life on the ocean wave'. Is he a friggin' mind reader? Or just as stupid as he looks.

Hang on a minute. In my defence, I don't read newspapers, I don't watch TV. How am I supposed to know about all this hat business? And it's the truth, tell the truth, there's still leniency out there, surely. Can't bend the truth, right. Well now, I have a legitimate excuse for not keeping up with current affairs. If it all goes tits up, at least I've been honest; ignorant maybe. Is ignorance a reasonable excuse?

The sound of keys jangling comes from down the corridor. Clank goes a cell door. Sounds like two or three cells away. We give each other a desperate glance. Everyone looks doomed.

Our door creaks open and we're each handed our mobile phones. The surly guard tells us we can make a three-minute call to inform our next of kin of our predicament. It's like we're being given our last rites. I hadn't seen my folks for a couple of weeks or so. I live across the other side of town. When I say my folks, I have a brother and sister. I call my sister, no answer. I call my brother, no answer. Three bloody minutes and no one's answering. Then my sister calls back. First thing she says, "Why do you always phone me when I'm powdering my nose; why?"

"So, listen, Sis," I say, telling her of my situation, blah, blah, she unsympathetically scorns me.

"Don't you ever read the newspapers or watch TV?"

"Uh, this is great, Sis, no, I don't. Is that a crime? I'm in a real fix here, and all you can do is give me earache. I'm up before the beak with minutes to spare. He's going to ask, 'What am I?' What am I going to say? What am I going to do? What *can* you do?"

"What can *I* do," she laughs.

"Er, yeah, hello, was that an echo? I just asked *you* that question."

"Don't get a hair up your ass with me," she says. "You've only got yourself to blame. You shut yourself away in that apartment, not knowing what the hell is going on in the outside world, living like a hermit. You don't even know what day it is half the time. Just scribbling down your little ditties and blowing your harmonicas day in, day out."

Bzzz, beep, end of call.

Well, that told me. That was great, very constructive. Thanks a bunch, shit! I'm thinking myself lucky she's not the judge.

"Phones! Now! Hand 'em in," the guard demands.

"Can I call my brother?" I ask.

"You've had your three minutes. Put your phone in the box," he orders, "You're up before the beak in one hour." That's it, I'm screwed. Okay, here we go. The penultimate destination.

Chapter 7

I'm led up the stairs and into the courtroom. A packed gallery, this time a different array of hats. It's like a fashion parade, a milliner's paradise. I don't recognise what half of these hats signify or identify with anyway, haven't got a clue. I could have put anything on my bonce the day they picked me up. Looking at this lot, I coulda got away with wearing a knotted handkerchief, imitated Michael Palin, and muttered, "I gorra pain in the brain." Well, too late now.

"All rise," shouts the clerk. Here he comes, my nemesis 'wig-man'. At least he's not wearing a black cap.

"Be seated."

"Defendant, rise."

"Champagne," he barks. The old git's said it again.

"It's *Shane Paine*, m'lord," says the clerk, correcting him.

"Mr Paine, I trust you're here this morning to inform the court 'what you are'. What do you have to say in your defence," hurrying me along.

"Yes!" Mmm, clearing my throat, I begin by saying, "Sir, I apologise for taking up the court's time. I was ignorant to the fact any law on hats had been proposed or indeed passed, due to the fact I don't go out much. I don't read newspapers and don't own a TV. So, I am unaware of everyday news."

This raises quite a gasp and a giggle in the gallery, as if it were the strangest thing they'd ever heard. Am I really the oddball here? I must be, looking at this lot, who seem astounded by my lack of interest in the media.

"Quiet!" the beak orders. "Go on, continue, Mr Paine."

"Yes sir, well sir *(three bags fuckin' full sir!)*, when I return to my home, I shall immediately endeavour to find my vocation in life or some affiliation, and immediately wear the appropriate hat."

"Mr Paine, all things considered, you have failed to comply with the law, having had ample time to make up your mind. You will not be returning to your abode, Mr Paine, ignorance is not an excuse. I sentence you to three months on the offshore colony for 'Men Without Hats'. Take him down."

"But, but," as I'm manhandled out of the courtroom, I'm passed by one of the morons with whom I shared a cell, being escorted in.

"No, no, this cannot be. What's going to happen to all my crap," I scream at my guard.

"That'll all be taken care of," he says. "Your next of kin will be informed."

Three months! Three fuckin' months. Why in God's name didn't I go down the Sally Army route? I could have been out on the street by now, in my hat and tunic, collection box in one hand, waving a tambourine in the other, singing, 'Come All Ye Faithful.' Why the hell didn't I try that? Too late now, as I'm escorted back to my cell to join the others.

I'm informed by my handler that I'm to be shipped out tomorrow, once I've had my medical, been deloused and deemed fit for purpose.

I ask my cellmates, "What's happened to the other moron who went up before me. Surely that idiot didn't come up with a convincing line and get one up on us. How?"

"No," came a reply, "he's in the local infirmary. The fool's jumped out of an open window without looking, hit the tarmac two floors down, busted himself up real bad."

I guess that's one way of avoiding the colony.

Then back to the cell comes the other moron who previously sang, "A life on the ocean wave."

So, his wish has come true, bless him.

Chapter 8

Head in my hands, I'm beginning to realise the enormity of it all, in between thinking pointless stuff like, did I put out the trash, turn off the bathroom light? All irrelevant crap, considering.

Early next morning, we're given our daily bread, taken out of the cell and marched down to an examination room, told to strip off and wait for the nurses. Ears, eyes, nose throat.

"Say ah, bend over, cough."

What a job. They meet more assholes in one day than regular folks do in a lifetime.

"Dust him down."

"Here's your bag," says a nurse at the first checkpoint.

Inside is soap, shampoo, toothbrush and paste, razor blade, can of foam, and a notebook and pen. And then we're led into kind of a salon to have our heads shaved, which I do anyway. But I can imagine it would be quite a shock for someone with a full head of hair.

I recall when I was in my twenties. I had a couple of friends (yes, really!). Trevor, one of them, lucky mutha, tall, dark, handsome, babe magnet, full head of thick wavy hennaed shoulder- length hair, that any woman would scratch your eyes out for. A dead ringer for Jim Morrison of 'The Doors'.

The other friend, Paul, great guy.

We're out together one night playing pool. Paul was bald as a coot, totally bald by the age of twenty, and this was the early seventies when hair really was the groove. We're chattin' away and he mentions Trevor, outa the blue. Paul rants, "I hate that bastard."

"Who?" I say.

"Trevor," he replies.

"Why? Wassup? What's he done to you?"

"Him and his precious hair," he says. "Shane, I've spent a fortune on my hair, trying to keep it; this lotion, that cream, potions and pills, anything and everything, and I'm bald at twenty, man."

I wanted to laugh out loud, but I could see he'd got a real problem with his follically-challenged bonce.

"That twat, Trevor," he continues, "washes that mop once a month under the cold water, sink tap, with a handful of fuckin' Persil washing powder. Whad'ya think about that then? Work that one out."

Oh my God, I coulda rolled around the floor laughing my ass off, but this was a real sensitive issue. So, I just managed a little frown and changed the subject.

Okay, that's the medical sorted. Got my bag of goodies. Last port of call is where I'm given a black jogging suit, two sizes too big. When I query it, I'm told they are one-size-fits-all, and a pair of flip-flops. My clothes and a few quid are bagged up and put in a locker for when, or if, I return.

Back in the cell, daunting trepidation mounts. Only four of us now. None of us had heard of this colony for 'Men Without Hats', before we arrived here. So, we're all imagining some terrible place, horsewhipped every day (that could be stretching the imagination somewhat), but who knows, it could be similar to the place portrayed in the movie 'Papillon'. That would be the worst scenario, worse than death. What a movie. Shut up in a hot shit-hole, hell, 24/7, no light, no air, mashing up in a tin cup any bugs venturing into the cell, to get a little protein. Just thinking of a place like that makes my skin crawl. But McQueen never lost the will to make his escape. Snap out of it. It was only a movie. This is like a movie. One minute I'm about to buy groceries, next minute I'm banged up, going Christ-knows where, with a bunch of strangers, who are as clueless as myself.

Chapter 9

It's hot in here, claustrophobic, smelly. The smell of panic and stress and unwashed bodies. A couple of guys look as if they're about to freak out and have a fit or a panic attack. I'm thinking of something I can say to ease the tension; less-than-relevant words fail me, and I end up saying,

"Listen guys, everything's gonna be alright." The Bob Marley mantra, 'it'll be alright,' famous last words. Will it? I don't know. Hadn't got a clue. But the guy sitting next to me seconds the mantra and joins me in saying, "Yeah, sure, it's going to be fine" (wasn't sure if he was being facetious), "we'll all be out of here in a jiff," he says. And once he'd confirmed my words, I saw their thoughts wander in another direction, and their fidgety bodies relax a little, panic over for now.

We're all sitting on the floor, backs against the wall. The air is calmer now. I'm closing my eyes, falling asleep, hoping I will awake in my own place, continuing my daily routine, but before I drift to that place, the cell door clanks loudly open, and we're handed our final slop before getting transported to wherever we're to embark.

Here we go, back into the same windowless van we arrived in, handcuffed together, just in case someone decides to do a runner. There's no view, so we've no idea where we're being delivered.

Half an hour or so later, we step out of the van to see a small dock. Anchored is a small barge, the kind you would see on a canal, awaiting us, and we begin to climb aboard, still handcuffed. The moron's face lights up with excitement – he thinks he's getting on The Royal Yacht Britannia. Like he's never been let out of his cage in years. He's lapping it up. Wow! The look of glee on that idiot's face. In a strange way, I'm envious of his excitement.

We're waiting for a few more folks to arrive, and here they come. Once everyone's checked in and we're seated, we get on our way. Chugging steadily out of the estuary. No landmarks. So, we've still no idea where we are. And then the moron from my cell, who I'm unfortunately handcuffed to, begins to sing. "Row, row, row your boat gently down the stream," and before he continues with, "merrily, merrily," I deliver him a sharp elbow in the ribs. I don't think this guy is ever coming back, and he may not even get there yet. I swear, if he breaks out into another kind of sea shanty, I'll kick the idiot overboard. Oh shit, I'm still handcuffed to him. Jesus, if I'd been told that I'd be sharing a room with him, I'd have taken us both over the side already.

After about an hour, we're cruising slowly to our docking point. A dock-hand grabs a thick coiled rope, ready to sling to this guy on shore, looks like a giant of a man who would be capable of lifting the boat right out of the water, with hands like size 12 shovels. The closer we get, the bigger and scarier he becomes, the biggest guy I've ever seen. I do believe he could be the missing link, or Cro-Magnon man. His features very ancient, undershot jaw, prominent forehead, deep-set eyes, bushy black eyebrows, five hairs short of meeting in the middle. You wouldn't want to rattle his chain. If he doubles up as a disciplinarian here, we're all screwed.

What a relief to step on *terra firma*. I was starting to feel the slop I'd consumed earlier, trying to resurface. Never did have sea-legs. My Pa was in the navy and that's one thing I didn't inherit from him. I once took a booze cruise from Dover to Calais for the sole purpose of bringing back beer, wine and ciggies to sell on because they were so cheap.

An old pal of mine, Ken, joined me on the trip. Big barrel-chested guy, Sean Connery lookalike, former biker. Arriving at the port in Dover, we're waved on up the ramp and onto the ferry. We park up and walk up onto the top deck to breathe in some fresh air, and then back down into the restaurant, where Ken orders two hearty English breakfasts, which I wasn't at all salivating for. Ken tucks in. I'm picking at a little of this and that, and suddenly, I can feel myself turning green. I get up to go up on deck to get some more fresh air.

Wiping his plate clean with his last piece of toast, Ken says to me, "You gonna leave that breakfast, kid?"

"Knock yourself out," I reply.

He takes my plate as I make a dash for the upper deck. I lean over the rails and proceed to spew up my guts. Aagh! Aagh! Christ, I felt awful, and we hadn't even left the bloody harbour. What was worse, we'd gotta come back. I was dreading it. Phew! That's a bit better. Can't remember eating that. So, with my head still spinning like a top, I go back down to the restaurant to join my old pal.

"How d'ya feel kid," he asks.

"Fucking terrible," I reply. "Thanks for asking".

"Spewed ya ring up, aint ya!"

"Yep, I sure have. How did you guess?"

"I'm sitting here," he says, "just finished your breakfast, looking out of the window. You must have been directly above me on deck. This debris, which could only be described as puke, comes falling past and was consumed by swooping seagulls before it could hit the water."

"Nice," I say, "a lovely day out in Dover, feeding the birds."

"How's about a nice cup of tea kid," he asks.

"That'd be great, Ken, happy days."

Chapter 10

"Come on, get in line," shouts a guy with a clipboard, who's checking us off the boat.

"You over here, you over there," as he allocates us into small groups.

I've got my fingers crossed behind my back, hoping and praying I'm going to be put with a group that can provide some mental stimulation. Maybe I'll be the thicko of the group and my *compadres* will be disappointed in me. Anyway, thank God the moron, my previous cellmate, is put about three groups away from me.

As we're led away, he shouts over to me, as if we've been best buddies all along, "See ya." I raise my hand to acknowledge him, thinking, "not if I see you first, pal."

Looking at my group, they don't look a bad bunch, but how can you tell? Part-time copper, Dennis Nielson, he looked respectable and intelligent, until he was discovered disposing of chopped-up body parts of young men down the drains. So, you never can tell.

We're shown to our dormitory. No bunks, great. Hate to be under some fat bastard farting away and rolling around all night. Just gets better. Surroundings outside don't look too bad either. Sunny day, few trees, benches, albeit a little cold. We're testing out our beds when in walks a Seargent Major-type guy, thick set, and the kind of voice you wouldn't want installed in your alarm clock. He bellows out the plan for tomorrow.

"Okay, listen up. Roll call 5.00am."

Uh, 5.00am, methinks. Never seen that time on a clock.

"Followed by shit, shave, shampoo-and-set, ladies. Exercise yard 6.00am. Anyone lagging will be put on latrine duties for a week."

That for me was encouragement enough to get my ass outa bed on time.

"Whilst exercising, you will be briefed on your daily activities and assignments, understood?"

"Hmm."

"UNDERSTOOD?" he demands.

"Yes sir," we reply.

He commands our attention and promptly leaves, slamming the door on his way out. We look around at each other and begin to introduce ourselves, seeing as we're going to be living together for the next three months. Well, some of us. Others seem a tad reticent.

Maybe some need a little more time to adjust. There's more than likely guys here who have been separated from their families, wives, kids. In a way, I'm lucky, I guess.

There are various posters on the dormitory walls, 'don't do this', 'don't do that', but one very prominent sign that was on every wall read, 'ON LEAVING THE DORM, YOUR HAT HUST BE WORN AT ALL TIMES'. And there it was, on the bedpost, a round, grey cap with a large red-letter T emblazoned on the front. T? Why T?

"Trainee, I guess," says the guy on the next bed to me.

"Trainee for what?" I reply.

"Who knows," he says. "We're gonna get some type of education, right!"

And the next morning, he was proved right. Trainees we were!

Morning, 6.00am, exercise yard. Star-jumps, press-ups, running on the spot, nothing too strenuous for thirty minutes, and then into the mess hall. No menu – of course not, but far superior to the previous slop we were served.

Once fed and watered, we're told to stand in line to receive a pamphlet, a questionnaire. Opening it up, and taking a swift glance, it seemed to ask some very silly questions. Obviously, a profile exam. I closed it and would read it a little later. The day passed quickly; it was early days. Maybe they'll drag later on. I hope not.

Back in the dorm, I'm lying on my bed, thinking about my life before, that had been taken from me. I realise I need to look ahead to stop me losing the plot. I take out the pamphlet from my bag. First question; favourite colour, RED maybe? Hmm! Could be associated with anger. Three favourite songs; WOW! Far too many genres I like so much; depends on one's mood, okay, maybe a 'Soft Cell' song, 'Nirvana' or a 'Sex Pistols' track. Nah! I could be seen as an angry, gay, suicidal anarchist, not exactly your average Joe. What's middle of the road? Yeah! Of course, 'Middle of the Road', Chirpy bloody Cheep Cheep, ha ha!, time to go to sleep.

Chapter 11

Next morning, after exercise and breakfast, we're ordered to follow an appointed Group Leader. How were they given this job? Who are they? How important are they? Would they be Head Boy or Milk Monitor at school? They're wearing blue hats emblazoned in yellow, that state 'Helper'. Helper? Help me get the hell outa here; could be a subtle ploy. You have a problem; you tell your helper. He files your complaint, and next minute your ass is hauled away somewhere never to be seen again. No. I don't think I'll ask for any help just now, thanks. I'll just observe for the time being to see who, when and how someone else gets it in the neck.

Today feels like the grand tour. We're led into another small hall. There's a giant TV. screen at the far end wall and a couple of stacks of white plastic chairs waiting to be picked up and placed in front of it, and we're seated. The helper has the remote, of course. We're all sitting comfortably. The TV is turned on and who should appear on the screen, Lorraine bloody Kelly. Incessant TV. presenter forever and a day.

"No, please no," mutter a few under their breath, voicing their displeasure.

"Quiet," says the helper, "you're spoiling it for the rest of the group."

Oh really?

What's with the This Morning TV thing? Are we expected to enjoy it? And if this is considered 'the norm', do we just pretend to enjoy it, like good little boys? And anything else we're not happy with, do we protest or abstain? I'm going to plump for the latter; neutrality. Keep *stumm*, keep the peace. We're being observed. The owners of this world want anaesthetized natives. We're being sussed out right now by people watching us watching TV, asking, "Does he conform? Is he easily pleased? Does he have a rebellious nature?" This whole facility has CCTV apart from the toilets and showers, I'm assuming.

I was a little naive before, thinking we were here just to choose a hat, but no, there's a cunning agenda here; thinly disguised, or am I being paranoid? One wasted hour of my life already, watching this drivel. I'm thinking, could Chinese water-torture be any worse? Of course it could.

I get immersed in my own little amusing thoughts about Lorraine, and wonder if her husband has ever thought of putting a plastic bag over her head, just to shut the silly cow up for five minutes. He's probably refused to have hearing aids numerous times. I'll wager she yaps the hell away even when they're bangin'. Yes, the credits start rolling and there's a commercial break.

Thank God for that. Now, maybe a movie, any movie or documentary. No such luck. It's Pipsqueak Schofield and Hollow Wallaby. Phil and Holly, the nation's darlings. The sickliest pair of plastic pricks on TV., just pipping rivals Eamonn and Ruth to the post. Another opinionated, cringeworthy couple of no consequence.

I must be blind – how stupid am I? I know what this is all about now, cutbacks. They want to see how many of us top ourselves, unable to consume any more dishwater. Really amusing myself now. This must really be getting to the serious souls. Those who don't have the mind for self-amusement. Wonder if we're going to be bombarded with this futile crap, day-in, day- out. But I can only amuse myself for so long before my sanity begins to wane. Anyway, one day down, mostly watching crap on TV. One down, eighty-nine to go. If this is the daily routine, it's hard work without lifting a finger.

Back in the dormitory, a few of us quietly discuss our first day, and the circumstances of how we got here in the first place, taking into account we were 'hatless' at the time. Two of the inmates were very quiet. They hadn't uttered a word since we'd been here. Okay, it's only the second day. I hadn't seen them arriving on the boat either. These guys stand out by being discreet. I'm assuming they know each other, but not seen them engage in any conversation. Could be spies planted amongst us. Or is my suspicious nature working overtime again? Everyone could be eyeballing me and thinking the same.

Chapter 12

Every morning, same routine. Exercise, breakfast, and then to the same hall. Oh no, not morning TV again. No. To my delight, great! Instead, we're each seated at small desks, all spaced out like we're about to sit a school exam, and handed a pen.

"Take out your questionnaire," instructs our 'helper'. You have one hour to complete the paper. Nine o'clock on the dot we begin, and pens down at ten on the dot. "Your pamphlets closed and returned to me," he adds. "Any questions not answered will lose you points. You will be downgraded and lose any privileges you have now."

Downgraded, loss of privileges; jeez! it could get worse. Didn't even realise we were upgraded. What privileges? Soap! Maybe? Shampoo, not a problem, got no hair.

I'd only flipped through this paper until now, totally unprepared. Seen only two of the inane questions, and they seem to get sillier as I look down the list, mostly asking one's favourites; likes/dislikes. Favourite movie, musical influences, food, drink, favourite time of day. What kinda stupid question is that? Yeah, if I was still at school, 'playtime', 'home time'. Phew! I could think about this one alone for ten minutes. Guess I'll put morning. It's when I discover I'm pink, with a pulse. That's a pretty good time of day. Easy now, I'm on a roll. Favourite news reader? Dermot, yes, Dermot Murnahan; always liked him. When I had a TV, top three TV hosts? This is it, I'm gonna dumb this right down. So, I answer, Lorraine Kelly, Philip Schofield, and his sickly side-kick, Holly Willoughby. Favourite weatherman? Weatherman? Okay, Michael Fish. Quote: "There will definitely not be a hurricane tomorrow." Well, that day you dropped a bollock, Michael. Thousands of trees blown over and eighteen folks killed. Favourite comedian: Bernard Manning. No. Too risqué, not at all PC. Jimmy Carr. Mm, another who's a tad too controversial. Alan Carr. Christ, no. He's got the voice that would crack a TV screen. I don't like either of them anyways. Ricky Gervais. Now, I like him, but he's mega controversial. Last I heard of him, he'd surrounded himself with a bunch of minders after receiving numerous death threats. I'll just put Ken Dodd. Never swore, never told a dirty joke. Would own the stage for four or five hours and watch members of the audience walk out through sheer exhaustion. It doesn't say if they have to be living or dearly departed. Movie: 'Sexy Beast', yeah, great movie. Hang on, it's a pretty violent film. Don't want anyone thinking I like a little violence, so forget that. 'Mary Poppins', that's harmless enough, or maybe I'll be seen as living in a fantasy world. A prime candidate for a lobotomy. How's about 'Shane', yeah, a good old family-values movie, 'Shane', yep, my namesake. I was mesmerised as a kid watching that movie. The vast landscape of the American West, amazing cinematography. 'Shane' it is then. I think I'm doing okay so far, for someone without a telly. All these are distant memories from when I used to have a TV and some contemporary snippets I've gleaned when visiting friends. Most TV personalities I used to watch are probably six feet under by now. Apart from the morning TV hosts, they've been going forever. I think they're friggin' robots on a loop. Right, favourite food: everything, more specifically, most everything. Okay, steak, just hope the markers aren't veggies. I'll answer muesli. Favourite drink: beer and beer. Or they could be teetotallers - I'll just put tea. This is getting tedious now. Next question. Musical influences: now this could be the dealbreaker. Am I gonna be honest? No. Most of my musical tastes have kinda anti-establishment lyrics, or something raunchy, nothing your grandma would like. It's gonna pain me to do it, I'm feeling like a traitor to myself, but I'm gonna put 'Barry Manilow', perfect! The polar opposite of a rebel. I think I've nailed that one. How'm I doin? I quickly revise my answers, twenty minutes to go. Favourite board game: Mm, another tricky question, 'Snakes and Ladders', harmless enough. 'Chess', my favourite, deep-thinking strategic, can't reveal that. Every few questions, there's a bit of a tricky one, subtly thrown in, building up a profile for the eye in the sky. I may be a terrible sceptic, but I'm certain we're not filling out this paper for fun. I'm into 'Online Poker' at the moment, love it; gambling, bluffing. I may be seen as bluffing my whole way through this place. 'Monopoly', yeah, game of luck; roll of the dice. Next, physical sports; easy, 'Tennis'. Although I do like 'Darts' and 'Snooker'. How can they be classed as a physical sport though, which I'm pretty sure they are now.

Remember, the Snooker player, Big Bill Werbeniuck. Pre-match, he'd warm up by washing down beta-blockers with about eighteen pints of lager. Never won a world championship; can't think why not. And the darter from north of the border, Jocky Wilson, who more often than not would approach the oche half pissed. I remember when he went down arse-over-tit, playing Eric Bristow in some final, and bounced right back up like a Weeble. Okay, I concede, quite physical. Long time ago now. Oh my, how we were entertained, pure top drawer. Ten minutes to go and I'm done. Keep it simple.

"Okay, time's up," says helper, "pens down, close your pamphlets now," he demands, looking at a couple of stragglers, seemingly stuck for an answer or two. "How d'ya do?" says a guy opposite me. I wasn't sure whether he was saying hello or asking me if I'd done okay, didn't ask him to elaborate, I just gave him a nod.

Chapter 13

We're into day four. We are about to go and find out what our assignments are to be. Based on, we're told, our hobbies, interests and any talents we may possess, eventually earning the proverbial cap that fits, or the hat, I should say.

The group have loosened up a bit now, and most of us are on first name terms. Some weird fish amongst us though, including myself. There's Steve, the steroid boy. He could pass for Cro-Magnon's son, very angry young fellow. I can see him kicking off when he's deprived of his next testosterone fix. It'd take at least all of us to subdue him, if he did. Walks around like 'Johnny Big Bollocks' all day, just looking for a scrap, so he can prove himself. You gotta wonder to yourself, what goes on inside that twat's head? What headgear is he gonna end up wearing? A big wet sponge with electrodes attached more than likely. One to avoid. And then there's Pete, the guy in the bed next to me. He's whimpered himself to sleep for the past three nights. Jeez, man up, I'm thinking, get a grip. I say to him, nobody wants to be here. It's only a matter of time and we'll all be back home. Initially, I thought he seemed okay and maybe we would get along, and maybe we still could, if he gets his head together. But he seems to be getting more and more fragile by the hour. I'm thinking he should be on suicide watch; God forbid. Think I'll have a sympathetic word in his ear later, try and calm him down a little,

There's an idea. I could train as a counsellor, work part-time for the Samaritans. Nah, second thoughts, I have enough problems of my own, and nobody listens to me, not even my sister, bless her. Samaritans? It's a thought. It's got to be a satisfying job, just knowing you may have pulled someone back from the brink, only to go on and suffer another day. And then there would be the sorry-ass attention seekers, someone phoning in to say they've been spreadeagled across the western line for over an hour now and there's a rail strike on, for Christ's sake. Or an old lady crying, she can't face another day since her Pomeranian passed away. What advice would I give this pair? I could tell them on the train track that the buses are still running, and I'll pop a timetable in the post. And tell the old lady maybe she should get another Pom or consider getting little 'Pepe' stuffed, then she and her little inanimate pooch could watch 'Good Morning' with Lorraine, together. I'm not sure I have the compassion required to do counselling. My number's been announced. I go to my assignment appointment. I sit in a cubicle, face to face, with a 'helper', eager to get me on a programme.

"Mr Paine?"

"Yes, Shane Paine, you can call me Shane."

"Mr Paine," he declines first name terms, "have you given any thought," he says, "as to what you would like to be, or do worthwhile with your life once you return to the mainland? We can put you on a course of your choosing, provided you have the aptitude. Work hard to earn your hat, then with a little guidance, become a valuable member of the community, who knows," he goes on, "even a pillar of society." Now I think he may be taking the piss.

"Indeed," he says, "judging from the marks you received on your questionnaire, I'd say you could possibly aspire to being a 'helper' right here on the island, helping the other unfortunate souls amongst us, who've fallen by the wayside."

Wow! I think it sounds like I've passed the test with flying colours. Mediocrity seems to work here then, just keep it simple. If I play my cards right, given time, I could be wearing the same hat as this guy, whoopee doo. I don't think so. Thank God we weren't given a truth serum before the assessment; I'd be buried here.

"Okay, sir," I say to the 'helper', "how long have I got to consider my options and really think about what I can do, what I want to be, so that I can come back here, say to you without any reservation, what I want to contribute?" I'm really sucking up to him now, kinda motivated by the faith he seems to have in me.

"One week from today," he replies, "the courses begin, so decide before then, and then there's always work detail."

Work detail? I enquire,

"Yes," he says.

"Anyone unable to decide on a training programme come next week will be deemed a failure and assigned to manual labour, and some, Mr Paine, never leave." What a daunting prospect, that's push enough for me to get my ass in gear.

"Since I've been here, I've only seen the inside of this compound, like everyone else. It's an isolated routine."

"Work detail? Hmm!"

We didn't see a chain gang on the way here, busting up rocks. Maybe it just involves cleaning up crap around here every day, he didn't elaborate.

Back in the dorm at the end of a fruitful day, I feel as if I've earned a stripe, gained a few brownie points. I may be getting ahead of myself here. I've still no idea what I want to be. There's always the last resort, a 'helper', but that may not get me off this island. I want to get back to all my creature comforts, my music, my writing, daydreaming, my own company. Nothing to think about, only myself all day, but that's not going to happen now anyway. Once I've decided what stupid hat goes on my bonce, I'll undoubtedly have a job. I have to think long and hard about this now. What job is going to suck up as little time out of my life as possible? One week seems ample time to make what should be a relatively simple decision. Dozens of options, but I'm reluctant to plumb for any job that requires eight hours a day, five days a week, having had all the time in the world to myself for the last five years. That's partly due to receiving an insurance pay-out and disability allowance for a motorcycle accident, in which I sustained a couple of injuries that limit my physical activities. And whoever said "Everything happens for a reason" was talking a load of bollocks.

Chapter 14

I'd purchased a 1,000cc Kawasaki ZL Eliminator motorcycle six weeks prior to the accident, a beautiful long, low, mean machine, quicker than shit off a shovel in a straight line. However, come manoeuvrability around the bends, it handled like a supermarket shopping trolley, but it looked great.

One sunny day, I decided to treat myself to a new armoured jacket. So, I set off on my two wheels to a motorcycle shop about ten miles away, tootling along on a dual carriageway, not more than forty miles per hour on the outside lane. I was head-to-head with a car being driven by a very old guy when, in the blink of an eye, he moved into my lane, clipped the lefthand side of my handlebars, catapulting me into the air and hitting the tarmac on the other side of the carriageway, sliding into the oncoming traffic. Everything's in slow motion. My wheels scraping the road, sparks flying. The bike is about three metres in front of me. We're both going to make contact with a high kerb. The bike hits it and bounces about ten feet up in the air, it comes down with a mighty crash just a few feet in front of me. That lump of metal weighed just under a quarter of a ton. Had it landed on me, I would have been mincemeat for sure. All the traffic came to a halt. It's like a bad movie. The old guy driving gets out of his car, walks over to me, looks down at me on the roadside. I'm writhing in pain, and he says nonchalantly, "What on earth do you think you were doing, uh?"

If I could have got up, I'd still be doing time for murder. Anyway, that limits my work options. Can't drive, operate machinery, climb ladders, etc. I have to make a list of jobs that doesn't incorporate any of these tasks, for starters.

There's a little banter going on in the dorm. I decide to throw something into the mix, see if I can get some positive feedback. A few ideas maybe, but nobody seems serious about the task at hand. No one seems to have a plan. You know what, I gotta take care of me, Numero Uno.

I don't think they'll realise until the last day, the big decision they have to make or else receive the shit end of the stick 'work detail'. So, I make myself heard and explain the reality of it all to them. To my amazement, they hadn't even been informed of the work detail they faced if they didn't get their brains in gear, and train for something for their ticket out of here. There was silence. You could cut the air with a knife. Blood drained from a few faces.

"What is work detail?" I'm asked.

"Dunno, manual labour of some kind," I replied. "I shouldn't imagine it's going to be a picnic. My 'helper' told me some of the 'work detail' people never leave this place."

It appears no one here had put as much thought into the questionnaire as myself. They had probably been totally honest or written down the first thing that had come to mind, and, because of the answers I had given, I stood out as a nobody, and somehow was privy to this 'work detail' deal.

Suddenly, everyone started flapping, "we gotta do this, gotta do that."

"Calm down," I say, "we have one week to get this sorted. If we all get our heads together, we'll be fine."

Then Pete, looking as fragile as ever, whimpers in confidence, "do you really think so, Shane?"

"Yes, Pete," trying to reassure him, "stop worrying," I say, "you'll be fine," consoling him, but unconvinced myself.

"Screw 'em," snarls Steve, "I'll just bust the hell outa here," ever nearing the need for his steroid fix.

Oh no, no way is he going home, he's gift-wrapped for a psychoanalyst.

Two rather shifty looking guys in the dorm, Derek and Paul, who I'd been observing earlier didn't say much to anyone in the group, and only kinda whispered to each other, which raised my suspicions. Occasionally, I would ask them how they were. Friendly questions like: Married? Kids? But always got back a nod or a monosyllabic answer. Could they be on the inside? I ask myself. Spies? I won't mention this to anyone else here, especially Steve. He's not the listening type. Subtle as a sledgehammer. He's liable to run over to them like a shot and crack their heads together. No, I'll keep my thoughts to myself for now, but I will force a little conversation on them at a later date, if they don't begin opening up a little.

Pete seems to be hanging on by a thread and on my coat-tails – he's like my shadow. I'm no mentor, I'm struggling here myself. I'm really not the one to give him any sound advice. Hell, the only decent advice I ever had was don't sleep under a coconut tree, which, of course, was a metaphor I didn't understand at the time.

Chapter 15

Talking of advice, I remember the Careers Officer who came to our school to offer advice to us final-year students, and the possibilities open to us, which in truth, were pretty slim. This was a secondary modern school for boys; school motto; 'spare the rod, spoil the child.' I hated it. Most of the teachers were sadists who obviously hated us, and also being there.

I'd been good at art, came top of the year a couple of times, "loved to draw and paint" I told the Careers Officer. He suggests there's a good chance he could get me a draughtsman apprenticeship at the local steel factory. Er, no thanks, I think, 'art that ain't'.

The school really was just for churning out factory fodder, to work in the many local industries in the area. We were all here because we'd all failed what was called the eleven-plus exams. Passing would have been a ticket to grammar school, which some would agree increased your success in life dramatically.

Corporal punishment in school back then was the norm. The cane, six of the best, either across your arse or your hand. Some sympathetic teachers would occasionally give you a choice. A wooden blackboard cleaner would often be flung blindly by a teacher across the classroom, bouncing off anyone who happened to be in its way. Or clipped around the ear on a daily basis just for being there. Three teachers, in particular, stood out for being very strict and downright bullies. All the time kids were being thrashed around the head, hit on the side of the head with a hardback; Christ knows how any of us weren't hospitalised.

We were little bastards, there's no denying it. One day we're in the classroom waiting for the Religious Education teacher to arrive. We were playing up, shouting, screaming, banging desk-lids, when in marches Mr Tipper, the Deputy Headmaster, ex-major or something. He'd made his own little cane, a stick about two feet long. He'd wound silver and red tape around it, making it look like a stick of Blackpool rock, and every step he took down the corridors, he'd slap the side of his leg with it, and if you happened to be passing him, he would strike out at your calf or shin. So, anytime we saw him coming towards us, we'd stick to the side of the corridor walls.

He's livid, screaming "quiet, silence". We all calm down and shut up.

"Pugh," he shouts, "Pugh," he calls for the second time, "get out here."

Graham Pugh, probably the most well-behaved and quietest kid in the school replies, "Sir, I haven't done anything."

"Get out here now, Pugh," Tipper yells.

Now Graham was also the biggest and most mature lad amongst us; muscular, hairy; he was already shaving at fourteen-years-old, and had sideburns like Elvis Presley. He says to old Tipper again, "No sir, it wasn't me, I've done nothing," and he hadn't.

Tipper made his way over to Pugh's desk, waving his little stripy stick, and physically stands Pugh up, walks him to the front of the class and orders him to hold out his hand and receive six of the best to make an example of him. Again, Pugh protests, "No sir".

Tipper's fuming, "What, boy! What!" He grabs Graham's left hand, holding it out. Tipper raises his cane to deliver his straight six, and before it can make contact with Pugh's palm, Graham gives him a right hook, bang on the chin, right on the button, his gold-rimmed glasses go ping, and fly across the classroom as he's going down like the proverbial sack of shit on the floor, spread out, spark out. Oh my God! Never seen anything like it. We all went crazy, chanting "Pughy, Pughy". There was uproar.

In rushed three teachers who'd heard the commotion. They picked up Tipper by his arms and legs and carried him out. What a place, my formative years. How I don't miss them. And yes, Graham Pugh was appointed teacher's pet after that episode.

Chapter 16

Into the second week, we're given a one-hour session with a helper to advise us on which course to follow, best suited to our abilities. The remainder of the days were spent just idling away. Some were kicking around a ball, a couple playing draughts. I was looking on when a guy from my dorm, Michael, came over to me, very overweight, big fat face. "Hi," he says, "enjoying the entertainment?" I nod. I hadn't really spoken to him before now.

"Whatcha doin'?" he asks.

I wasn't doing anything, as he could see. Couldn't he gather that. So, I respond with a glib remark and say,

"Oh, just playing a game of 'I Spy' with myself," expecting a wry smile. A look of bewilderment crossed his face.

"Uh," he says, "really, how do you do that?"

Oh dear! Is he serious? I'm thinking yep, he is.

Then who walks over, the moron, with whom I'd once shared a cell, also named Michael, I'd since learned. I introduce them to each other, praising them up equally.

They walk away, buddies already, talking bullshit no doubt. They'll get on like a house on fire.

Back in the dorm, I do a head count, try and isolate any brains amongst us. There's steroid Steve, one down; whimpering Pete, two down; 'I Spy' Michael, three down – five of us left so far, including myself, with, I hope, some measure of grey matter.

Time is passing quickly in anticipation of the big decision day. How time flies when you're dreading something. I have a few ideas floating around in my head, but nothing I've thought of yet to get me a four-hour working day or less. We have no contact here with the outside world, not that I was interested in what's going on anyway. There's no news when the TV's turned on after breakfast, just three hours of mind-numbing drivel, if you're interested. How to make the perfect cupcake, what is the must-wear summer collection, and who's the latest Hollywood star to have an ass-lift. Not news at its zenith, but many, sadly, would disagree.

You know what I'm thinking? Counselling, helping, I keep going back to that idea, a helpline. Could I get a telephone installed? I could work from home, surely there wouldn't be back-to-back calls 24/7, one or two, maybe three calls a day, I don't know.

No idea how many people out there are going through a crisis. Doing that would be cool. It'd kinda get me outa the house, without leaving my armchair. I could carry on with my own life in-between calls. If any problems arose that I couldn't handle, I'd simply direct them to the right place. I may just meet some interesting people calling in, a novelist with writer's block because he'd punched the walls, short of ideas, and couldn't use his hands, a saxophonist who'd had his front teeth knocked out, a darts' player with *dartitis* – the inability to let go of the darts – a new diagnosis exclusive to darts' players, suffered by a previous number one, Eric Bristow. This could open up a whole new world for me. I could be a famous agony uncle, putting the world to rights, my own TV show, or at the very least, get a slot on morning TV and chat away with Lorraine Kelly, if I could get a bloody word in. But seriously, the more I think about this, the more excited I am about the idea. First thing tomorrow morning, I'll put this forward in my session with the 'helper'. Maybe I'm going over the top, but imagine my hat, a black cap, "Helper" embroidered in gold, wow! Yep, I've *already* gone over the top.

Next morning, after a restless night thinking about my proposed new vocation, I'm ready with a few mental notes to face my inquisitor. Right, just play it cool, throw in the idea, nonchalant, remind him of his suggestion to me about the possibility of being a helper for the needy, see how it goes.

"Good morning, Mr Paine," he says cheerfully. I'm never gonna be on first name terms with this jobsworth.

"Good morning 'Helper'," I reply, and go on to tell him I've decided to take his advice about training to be a 'helper' and contribute my services for the benefit of the nation, and others less fortunate. I ask, would it be possible for me to do this line of work on the mainland, telling him my idea of manning a Call Centre, a helpline service from my home, and then I begin to waffle on about already being of some comfort to a couple of unstable inmates whilst under arrest, here on the island.

"We don't refer to anyone here as inmates, Mr Paine," he interjects, "we prefer the term 'guests', just like McDonalds. And would you care to elaborate as to whom you have given any advice or comfort since you have been here."

"Well," I say, "I don't know any last names, but there's a chap in the next bed to me, Pete or Peter is his name."

"Peter Jones," the 'helper' says, "he left the island this morning".

"He's left already?" I ask, taken aback. "How? What hat has he earned in such a short time?"

"He didn't leave wearing a hat," was the reply. "He left in a box."

"What, a box?"

"A coffin, Mr Paine. Mr Jones took his own life during the night." So much for my words of comfort.

A wave of guilt washed over me; the poor guy, the stupid bugger. And then, I started to think about myself, pretending to be his friend whilst trying to shake him off my coat tails, telling him he'd be okay, when I knew he wasn't. Then, on reflection, I realise the limits of what anyone can do. What can you do or say to anybody a little unhinged? Not a lot, really. Poor guy.

"So, let's continue," says the 'helper.' "This is the way it works, to answer your question, yes, it is possible you can do this work when you return to your home, if you're sure this is what you want to do. You will spend the remaining time here with a team who will train you for the job of 'helper'. Sign here if you feel you're ready."

I'm thinking I'm as ready as I'll ever be, just let me get through this and get back to my comfort zone. Wow! I'm on the road, just have to get my head down now, and listen for a change.

Chapter 17

Back in the dorm, everyone seems to be in a lighter mood, discussions going on about the hats they'll be wearing for their chosen career.

Steroid Steve has plumbed to enlist in the regular army and will train alongside service men stationed on the island. Mm, I did say he's not the listening type. See how long he lasts before he's court-marshalled for getting his own regiment wiped out. I think it's a recipe for disaster, like giving a chimp an Uzi. Time will tell.

I'm actually missing Pete. Maybe I could have done more. Oh well, too late now.

Michael's gonna be a bus driver. That'll keep him from driving people up the wall, or not, ha ha. The two quiet shifty guys, Derek and Paul, aren't throwing anything in the mix. I'm highly suspicious of them. However, one would think, if they were on the inside, they would at least possess the art of conversation, to glean as much information as possible from each of us, but I don't know, strangeness isn't that scarce.

The two other guys in the dorm, Phil and Simon; Phil, sporty type, never keeps still – he'd survive in a four-by-four cell jogging on the spot. He's going down the fitness route, obviously, a defined, lean machine, marathon runner by all accounts. Why on earth didn't he give the arresting officers the slip and leave them standing, dunno. Then there's Simon, not at all simple. Wins at chess every time, finishes the censored daily rag, crosswords, sudoku, and puzzles in no time, a walking encyclopaedia, clever clogs, without any air of superiority, nice guy. What's he doing here? Got to have attended grammar school; the 'ask me anything' type. I've yet to engage any in-depth conversation with these two so far, but they seem okay.

I've been given some literature on basic skills for the course I'm taking. I need to begin revising and at least show a little interest and knowledge to whoever's my tutor. I start my course tomorrow and I'm actually a little excited.

Morning comes. I jump out of bed, I'm ready. Phil's already out in the exercise yard, always the first up, first out, and today, he's in charge of the daily exercise routine. The first day of his course, thirty minutes exercise with this whippet every morning. We're gonna be fit alright, fit for the knacker's yard.

Just finished my hearty breakfast. Always the same, porridge and a chopped-up banana with a drizzle of honey over the top. Off I go to where I'm greeted by my tutors. To my surprise, there are three more trainees in the group. We do a little preliminary paperwork and are led into a room with a few chairs and tables. At one table in the middle of the room there are two chairs facing each other. On the table there are two dummy cableless telephones.

"Okay," says one tutor, "who would like to go first?"

"At what?" I ask.

"Two of you," he says, "sit opposite each other at the table, each with a phone. One of you has the role of a caller with a problem. The other, the role of a 'helper', who will attempt to solve the problem. And then the roles will be reversed, got it?"

"Yes," we answer.

"Okay," he says, "let's get underway."

"What problem?" I ask.

"Ask any problem," he replies. Use your imagination. "So, who wants to go first as the caller and the helper? We will all take a turn and observe each other's reaction and response."

"Er, okay," I say, "I guess I'll go first. I'll be the caller," thinking this will give me a chance to see how the other guy responds. So, we take our seats. At that, a roller blind is lowered down onto the centre of the table, so we're unable to see each other's facial expressions.

"Okay, begin, caller," I'm told.

"Uh, okay." recalling an earlier thought I'd had about a saxophone player who'd had his front teeth knocked out. I pick up the handset and I have to say, 'ring, ring'. I think I'm going to crack up already. I can't keep a straight face.

"Hello," answers my counterpart, equally amused. "John West speaking, How may I help?"

"Well," I say, "I'm a saxophone player, at least I was, until I had a fall off my bike and knocked out my two front teeth. I'm now unable to make my living in a band singing and playing the sax. I'm very depressed, to the point where I've contemplated taking my own life."

"Oh dear," he replies. "Have you sought any help from a dentist, or your doctor? Maybe you could have a bridge made or have implants. I could refer you to a good dental surgeon".

I tell him, "I've already been down that route and that only implants would work because of the pressure of biting down on the sax mouthpiece, number one, I can't afford £3,000 for the implants, and number two, the whole process takes around six months. How do I make a living, in the meantime?"

"How about this," he says, "may I suggest when you play, wear a boxer's gum-shield."

Okay, I'm thinking, I'll string this along a little. "Maybe that's a good idea," I say, "which it *is* for when

I'm playing the saxophone, but how about when I have to sing."

"Simply take it out," he replies.

"Ah, that's where there's another problem," I tell him. "Having no front teeth has left me with a lisp, so when I perform my repertoire, I sing, 'you are my thunthine, my only thunthine' and 'Wake Up, Little Thuthie'."

At that my fellow students are laughing helplessly, but the tutors remain stone-faced and unfazed. My counterpart then suggests I change my song list. "Find out what song lyrics have little or no letters S or C," so that my lisp is diminished.

"Why don't you include," he says, "songs like, er, let's say that Jim Reeves number, 'Make the World Go Away'."

That also raised a bit of a giggle.

"Mr West," pipes up a tutor, interrupting our conversation.

"Yes," says West.

"That's hardly an appropriate song to suggest for someone who's considering meeting his maker, don't you agree?"

"Oh, yes," says West. "Sorry, I didn't think."

"Okay," says the tutor, "change roles."

"Ring, ring," says my counterpart.

I pick up. "Hello, Helping Hands Helpline" my own name for the line, "good, eh? Show a little initiative. Who may I ask is calling?"

"It's John, John West."

"Hello, may I call you John?"

"Yes, that's fine," he says.

"Okay, John, how may I help?"

"Well," he goes on, "I'm at my wits end. I get home from work last month to three unfed kids, all under eight-years-old, and no sign of my wife. They're being looked after by my next-door neighbour who hands me a sealed envelope and says, as she's leaving, "if there's anything I can do, you know where I am," and closes the door on her way out. The kids are watching TV as I open the letter. 'Dear John', classic. 'Dear John, I'm so sorry I'm leaving you. I'm sorry but I've fallen in love with Mary, our friend Mary, our relationship has been going on for over a year now, and I can't live without her. We'll sort out everything real soon with the kids and all, sorry. Signed Sarah.' " Clearing his throat.

Jeez! This sounds too real, I think this is true. It's either true or the guy's got a very vivid imagination. He's definitely put me on thin ice here. Think, think. What do I say? I look over at the tutors, I'm a little puzzled, but they're passive and await to observe my response.

"Hello," says John, "are you still there?"

"Yes, I'm still here, John," I reassure him. "I'm sorry for your situation. The first priority is the welfare of your children, right?"

"No shit, Sherlock," he replies, agitated.

"Uh, do they have any idea where or what has happened with their mother?"

"Yes," he explains, "she's visiting aunty Mary for a few days."

"Oh," I say, "so they're not upset or anything?"

"No!" he shouts loudly, "I'm the one who's friggin' upset. What the hell do I do now?"

I knew it, it's true.

The tutor steps in and walks a tearful John outside. Everyone's open-mouthed, gobsmacked, muttering, "oh shit."

John West is never seen in a session again. The first real problem he'd encounter is likely to tip him over the edge.

"I think we'll end this session now," says the other tutor, "and resume at ten o'clock in the morning, okay?"

Chapter 18

Back in the dormitory, we all have a chat about our daily activities. I notice Steve's not here. "Anyone seen Steve?" I ask.

Up pipes Simon, "Haven't you heard? He's in the can."

"The can, why? For what?"

"Yeah," he says, "he chinned the commanding officer this morning."

I knew it, we all knew it. He couldn't last one bloody day. We all rolled around laughing helplessly. He was an accident waiting to happen. Even Derek and Paul, the two quietly suspicious guys, were amused. It was the first time they had displayed any normality.

"Oh well, another eventful day at Butlitz," our pet name for the camp.

So now our group has been whittled down to six; myself, Michael, Phil, Simon and the two odd fellows, Derek and Paul. As time goes by, two weeks into our training, I believed I was making some good progress. We had another trainee in our course group to replace

John West. Who knows what's happened to him. When anyone's shipped out, there's never any news of their whereabouts. Nothing's been heard of Steve either. Maybe John's gone west; maybe Steve's gone south. Who knows? Who cares?

I used to think I hadn't got the time for a real job, but now I think I'm gonna enjoy juggling my own stuff, with my new vocation. We were all still well aware of the fact that we're observed and listened to on a daily basis. It's very difficult to behave naturally. There were times when one of us would slip up and say or do something we shouldn't have. It was unavoidable really, and we were to learn the consequences of this very soon.

We were each given an appointment to discuss this and that, a kind of assessment of our progress. This really was to expose any of us as charlatans. Going along with everything, just to get out of this place. Myself, I was going to give it my best shot, and had done so far. I wasn't worried at all that I'd done anything contrary to what was expected of me. However, at my interview, I was confronted with video and audio recordings of my behaviour, and everyone else's, and there it was, in black and white, so to speak.

My critical and cynical views on this place, the world and everyone in it, without excluding myself, but all that was documented before I began my training. So, I was given a stern warning by my interviewer and told that, especially with the course I was taking, any subversive nature would not be tolerated, so I received a verbal warning, the first and the last, he said. So, after that little upset, I endeavoured to be squeaky clean.

The interviewer then puts to me a casual unassuming question, unaware of my highly suspicious nature. "Have you had any rapport with the two fellows, Derek and Paul, in your dormitory?" he asks, "and have you observed anything untoward about them?"

Mm, that's way out of the blue. What is this? I wasn't gonna be some kind of informer for the people here, who were holding me against my will, and anyways, I can honestly say I've hardly exchanged a dozen words with them since I've been here, I told him. I'm keeping my trap shut, keeping my feet on neutral ground. But it was obvious they were of particular interest.

We're well into our training now. Feels almost like a proper job already. Going for exercise every morning, breakfast, training, lunch, training, dinner, dorm. I'm feeling good, fit, brains in gear. I'm feeling better than I've felt in years. Wish I could have brought my harmonicas though, and there's also a distinct lack of the fairer sex.

Simon's writing articles, developing puzzles, conundrums, etc. He's got a great sense of humour, dry, witty, this clever dick will get a hat with 'man with two brains' emblazoned on it. He's planning his own English version of the American 'Kiss and Tell' mag,

'The National Enquirer', "but extra sleazy, extra stupid," he says. "I'll run stories like: 'My husband had a sex change so he could be a lesbian, but now he's getting it reversed on the NHS,' or 'My pet gerbil picked my winning lottery numbers before he got eaten by the neighbour's cat, and now he won't be here to enjoy it'."

I'm sure it'll be read by millions, believed by many and have many more up in arms. Those who have been waiting for hip replacements for five years and a sack full of letters to the editor from 'The Gerbil Appreciation Society'. You couldn't make it up; well, you could. It should do well.

I remember Freddie Starr, a TV comedian, 'The Hamster Saga.' He always denied he'd eaten a live hamster in a sandwich, but the story ran for weeks, front page news of some red-top and was voted by readers as their favourite front page in fifty years of print.

Phil's daily exercise routines are getting harder by the day. I like him, but he's clearly mental. After thirty minutes with him every morning now, we're feeling physically sick. I think he's lying in bed every night thinking how he's gonna get us in the same shape as himself. That's never gonna happen. He's going to end up a drill sergeant for the marines probably, and watch them drop like flies, initiating a new recruitment drive.

Michael's training for the job he was born to do, sitting on his fat arse all day, driving an old charabanc full of rattling crash-test dummies around the island. He's put on weight since he's been here, despite Phil's punishing exercise routine. He's seeing more of this island than anyone. He'll probably stay here. He's very jolly and content. I can see him starting up his own company, organising mystery tours. He could be talking over the tannoy right now to his crash test dummies, perfecting his pitch. He doesn't have a helper on board looking over his shoulder. I'm not sure they'd want to risk it. He's just left to his own devices. Big happy-faced chap, he must be loving it.

One month down, and into our fifth week of training. The dormitory has got pretty claustrophobic. I think we're all starting to get a little cabin fever. Derek and Paul decided they're going down the ministerial route. No idea what congregation they've chosen; so many choices. How do these people decide which holy path to follow? I don't buy it; mumbo-jumbo, pseudo-nurture, we as a family never said grace before dinner. It was bought from the supermarket, courtesy of Ma and Pa working their asses off, not provided by some deity. I read that there are more than forty-five-thousand denominations in the world, so take your pick, the best one tailored to suit your needs. Alternatively, reach the age of reason already.

Some guy I once knew well, Bill, a Jehovah's Witness, now hawks his good book around the local town. I bump into him once in a while. We stop, have a chat about who's to blame for all the crap in the world.

He once said to me, "Shane, you've gotta believe in something."

"Why?" I asked. I didn't get a sensible answer. Twenty-five years ago, the only thing he believed in was a syringe. So now, I guess he's found the lesser of two evils. I could be wrong.

I have another good friend, he's Catholic. I won't hold that against him. He keeps it to himself. He knows my views on the subject, but on the odd occasion, he has to let it out. We worked together, played together. One time we're doing a job, I'm supposed to meet him early one morning. I can't find the keys to my van. I call him up, tell him I'm going to be late. "Alright," he says, "see you when you get here." One hour later, after turning the van inside out, there they were, down the side of the spare wheel. Is there anything more satisfying than finding your keys? I'm immediately on my merry way. I get on site, he's there to greet me.

"Found your keys then?" he says.

"Er, well, yes," I say, "I wouldn't be here otherwise."

Then he goes and ruins my day by saying, "I knew you would. I prayed to St Jude you'd find them." Amazing, a key-finding saint!

I bit my tongue and got down to work. I did send him a couple of YouTube videos featuring Christopher Hitchens, an antitheist who rubbishes religion in the most eloquent way. Don't know if he ever viewed them, probably not. Too brain-washed to even consider denial. Believers are so convinced they know something the rest of us don't? The devil buried dinosaur bones in the earth so sinners would believe in evolution. Right! Christopher Hitchens was once asked during a debate on religion if he'd ever prayed. "Only one time, for a hard on," he replied.

Derek and Paul, now a couple of bible-bashers carrying their bibles everywhere (religiously), seem very dedicated, quoting parables, verses and passages, testing each other's knowledge on the tooth fairy, to the point they're getting on everyone's tits and have been told to keep it a little quiet and read to themselves. We don't want to know. We don't want to be converted or saved just yet, thank you. The way they're going at it, they're aspiring to be either the Pope or the Archbishop of Canterbury – now there's an impressive pair of friggin' hats.

I just don't get religion. I'm fascinated by its magnetism, but far from convinced. I've spent some time in the USA and been quite entertained by some of the TV evangelists strutting their stuff, and at the bottom of the screen there is the Visa or Mastercard account into which you can send your gift or donation, with the promise of redemption.

It's pretty obscene; two of the most notorious preachers of piffle on TV were husband and wife, Jim and Tammy-Faye Bakker, presenting a show, (P.T.L.)

Praise the Lord. At the programme's peak in the late seventies, they were raking in one million dollars a week in donations. A private jet, multiple mansions, swanky cars, living the life of luxury, a kennel for their poodles the size of a house, fitted with central-heating and shagpile carpet, all financed by the easily led.

The following years I spent a lot of time in America, but my first trip was when I left school at fifteen-years old. My grandma always told me as a kid growing up, she would send me on a trip to New Jersey to visit my aunt, uncle and five cousins. My aunt had left England to be a nanny in New York when she was eighteen and never came back. What an eye-opener for me, fifteen years old, summer 1970, Ventnor, New Jersey, 119 North Swarthmore Avenue, forever printed in my memory, two blocks from the beach. Block after block of big amazing detached houses, manicured lawns, big cars on long drives, spotless wide roads, the polar opposite from what I'd just left behind; a terraced house on a rundown Council estate in the Midlands, the so-called Black Country, aptly named, sooty, grimy, industrial, remnants of coalmines peppering the landscape, nightly red skies glowing from opened furnaces of the steel plants. You needed to leave to realise just what a dump it was back then. These days it's not so bad, and I have to say, I'm very proud of my roots now. Especially the sense of humour.

My aunt was a theatre nurse and friends with quite a few highly-regarded surgeons and doctors. She was frequently invited to weekend afternoon pool parties at their sprawling mansions, and along I would go with her, my uncle and five cousins – happy days indeed!

I became good pals with a kid who had come down from New York to Ventnor for the summer break. Jaimie, the same age as me. His parents owned an enormous beach-front house on Washington Avenue, and at the end of his break, I was invited by him and his wealthy parents, to spend a week at their main home, a swish apartment in the prestigious United Nations Plaza. I was treated like a little prince, given the grand tour of NYC in a Cadillac limousine. Back at the Plaza one evening, I shared the elevator with Johnny Carson and Truman Capote. I was introduced to them by my hosts, not really aware of who they were at the time, but years later, I realised that was my only claim to fame.

I was having a ball and, of course, all good things come to an end. Six weeks later, I was back in old Blighty. I had to pinch myself to realise I had really been there. I was in the pits, determined to get my ass back across the pond as soon as possible.

I got myself a job and saved like hell. My dad was a great guy, he sang, played piano and accordion. He compered on musical nights held in the social club my parents used to manage. He'd get all the ladies' knees knocking with his rendition of 'Spanish Eyes'. He suffered a brain haemorrhage at thirty-two years old, which left him severely disabled. He couldn't work a decent paid job. So, we, my sister and brother, grew up without the proverbial pot to piss in, along with every other family on the estate. He said to me when I returned home, "So how was America, son?"

"Fantastic, dad," I said, "everyone's rich over there." In my naïveté, I asked him, "Why are we so poor, dad?"

He replied, "We're not poor, son, we're just broke." We laughed. He'd had part of his brain taken away, but hadn't lost his sense of humour.

It's six weeks into our training. Picking up our dummy phones, it's getting difficult now, thinking of a problem to present to the trainee helper. We're wracking our brains to come up with anything conceivable. No one's being super inventive, it's getting a little monotonous. This doesn't go unnoticed by the tutors, and at the end of the session, we're informed by them that four new faces will be joining the group tomorrow, and the four of us here will be manning the helpline only. New blood, that's what's needed.

Next morning, we're seated at our stations, anticipating the four new arrivals. Four tables have been arranged, positioned so that we have no visual idea of who we're supposedly helping. We hear them arrive and pleasantries are exchanged, we begin. One by one, problems anew arise, seeking some sound advice or guidance, which is very refreshing. But the session does get off to a slow start, problems the four of us wouldn't have dreamt up in a million years, like "I'm addicted to crisps" or "my right foot's bigger than my other one is." – He's been listening to Frank Zappa (Zombie Hoof). And then there's "I'm in big trouble, I was arrested the other night. I hit someone in a bar for saying Daniel O'Donnell was gay. I know that's not true," he says, "because my friend, a fellow fan, told me he'd seen a porno movie that featured a bloke who could have been his double, shagging a bird who looked like Susan Boyle's granny."

Mmm! this isn't going so well, but these problems have to be addressed, and it's proving more difficult than having the problem. Here I go, first up, with the bigger foot issue. I say to him, "you know, it's quite common to have one foot a little bigger than the other."

"No, no," he says, "you don't understand. My left foot is a size six and my right is a size thirteen."

Jeez, I think I'd like to see this.

He continues, "every time I need new shoes, I have to buy two pairs and throw one pair away. Everyone I pass in the street takes a good look at my feet and more often than not, make a hurtful comment, even other folks I know, who I've confided in, don't take me seriously, they just take the piss. I had a heart-to-heart with a so-called friend of mine not so long ago. He made a flippant remark; said I could get a job with Chipperfield's Circus, occupying the freak tent."

"Have you spoken to a doctor?" I ask.

"Yes, he says I was referred to a consultant a couple of years ago. There's really nothing they can do, except amputate one foot or the other. Then I'm left with the dilemma of which foot to have removed."

"Oh dear," I say, showing some concern, when I really feel like bursting out with laughter. I can hear my fellow trainees muffled giggles.

"Okay," I say, "I suggest you see a psychologist. Would you like me to get you a referral? Because I believe the biggest problem here is in your mind," which I really didn't believe.

"No, no, no, it's not," he retorts, "it's my big God-damned foot."

"Okay, calm down," I say, trying to reassure him. "We'll get to the foot of this, sorry, I mean the root of this. Let me book you in for another session." And he agrees. Phew!

Then over on the next table, my colleague attempts to deal with the Daniel O'Donnell issue. The caller begins, "I've been a lifelong fan of Daniel O'Donnell. I've been to County Donegal, Ireland, four times, waited for hours in a line of fans a mile long, just to be served a cup of tea by his mom at their family home; lovely, lovely, lady. He's the best singer in the world, you know."

"I didn't know."

"And the nicest man in the world," he adds. My colleague asks, "Oh, you've actually met him?"

"No, no, not yet," he replies, "but I will."

I'm thinking, I bet Daniel can't wait.

"How long have you had this obsession with Daniel?" he's asked.

"It's not an obsession," he says defensively.

"No, okay. Infatuation?" he suggests.

"No," he answers angrily.

"Okay! Okay!"

My colleague, now coming to a dead-end, asks, "Would you like to describe to me your connection with Daniel."

"Haven't you heard his music?" he responds, as if the whole world has his latest album 'The Best Of'.

"No, I haven't," says my colleague.

"Well," he recommends, "just listen to the track 'Footsteps Following Me," and then puts a little tune to the next line, "Footsteps, I cannot see."

Oh my God, this is great, pure gold, and is certainly giving me and my colleagues initiative, and more so, entertainment. We don't know if it's real or not, but it's priceless, and we're all doing our very best not to crack up.

He finishes off by saying he won't hear a bad word said against Daniel O'Donnell and asks should he plead guilty or not guilty to the assault charge, due to mitigating circumstances. He's advised by my colleague to plead the latter in the hope that the magistrate is also a fan of Daniel O'Donnell.

"Next!" announces the tutor.

"Crisps, I'm addicted to crisps," reveals the caller.

"Any particular flavour or brand?" asks my other colleague.

"Nah," he replies, "just crisps, any crisps."

"What is it with crisps?" he's asked.

"I just love crisps, breakfast, lunch, dinner, supper too, occasionally. And most days I snack in-between."

"Let me guess," says my colleague, "crisps."

"Yep," he says.

"What else? Is that all you ever eat?"

"Pretty much," he utters, "other than the odd Cheese Puff and a Wotsit or two. Now and again, I'll have a bag of Hula Hoops."

"Oh, so it's quite a varied diet really," says my teammate facetiously.

"Yes," he says, quite convinced.

"So, why are you calling the helpline today?" he asks. "You seem quite content with your eating habits. Are you ill?"

"No," he says, "my family have concerns for my wellbeing. They have a normal diet. My sister's a vegan and my brother's on the meat-only Atkins diet."

"Sounds like all your family have an eating dilemma."

"What do you mean?" he says, head in the sand.

"Okay," says my colleague, "I can refer you to a dietician if you wish."

"Will he stop me from eating crisps?" he gasps.

"No, of course not, no one can stop you eating crisps."

"I am going to make my diet a little more varied," he declares. "From today, in fact. I'll go and get myself a bag of Doritos right now; try and make some headway."

What a bunch, and I thought I had some issues. One more call to go. I give my colleague the thumbs up.

'Ring, ring'. Teammate No.4 picks up the phone. "Hello, how may I help you?"

"Well," the caller begins, "I want to remain anonymous for a start."

"Okay, that's fine, go ahead, what's the problem?"

"Well, I don't see it as a problem *per-se*. I have this obsession with death."

"You have a fear of dying?" he is asked.

"No, no," he says, "I like visiting morgues up and down the country, sneaking in at night and observing dead people."

We're all looking at each other thinking this is a strange one. They've saved the best till last. We're on the edge of our seats here, listening intently for what's coming next.

"Go on," says my colleague.

"Well," explains the caller, "I look at them for a while and then I like to lie beside them, cuddle them, hold their stiff hands, kiss their cold faces, and speak to them."

"And," asks my colleague, "do they ever talk back to you?"

"Yes, all of them," he exclaims, "all of the time, every one of them."

"And what do they say?"

There's total silence in the room, and then he screams out, "GET THE FUCK OUT OF HERE! They say, I'm trying to get some peace," then bursts out laughing hysterically. And that brings to an end the day's session of Loony Toons.

Chapter 19

The callers leave, and we remain with the tutors to discuss the day's session. They tell us, the callers today are four of the many so-called 'failures' on the island that are very unlikely to ever leave, due to, I'm sure you've observed mental issues. And he adds, "When you return to the mainland, you will experience many more similar, problematic calls from some people incapable of contributing anything worthy to society, and it will be your duty, once you have earned your hat and become qualified helpers, to gain the callers' confidence, pinpoint their location, and then report any such misfits to your superiors."

The realisation of what my job is going to be hits me like a brick full in the face. I've been training to be a spy. We're going to be spies, snitches, filtering out and reporting social rejects. I've been groomed as a snoop for the man all along, since the day I sat down with the 'helper', I signed in with, cajoled by him, giving me all the spin. Now I'm feeling pretty duped and stupid. Yes, I could have screwed up filling out the questionnaire, and maybe ended up as experimental fodder, like the four callers just now. I can feel all enthusiasm for this job draining from me. What am I doing? I really believed I was doing something good and worthwhile.

I bring myself around, out of my dizzy thoughts. I realise I have to continue now and keep up a charade to get myself out of this place. So, I will persevere, get my head down and do what's expected of me, and once I'm back home, I'll play this game by my own rules.

One more week to go. I've lost count of how many unfortunate head-cases we've interviewed, most of them without a snowball's chance in hell of ever getting out of here. It's a madhouse for sure, and if we all made our thoughts public, we'd all end our days in this place. I'm making the most of the cards I'm holding, hoping no one calls my bluff.

We're all back in the dormitory now. Everyone's present, Derek and Paul, the bible bashers, Michael, the bus driver, fitness-freak Phil, Simon Encyclopaedia-Britannica and myself, Mr Gullible.

They all seem cool, calm and collected, content in what they think the future holds for them. There's nothing for them to really think about. Nothing to get concerned over, only the job at hand that they have trained for. No getting into anybody's mind of troublesome thoughts.

Things aren't so clear-cut for me. I have to actually employ my conscience from the very first phone call I receive. My phone could be tapped. What if I do get some fruitcake on the line that I fail to report, or try to get them out of the trap they're about to set for themselves by confiding in me their innermost thoughts, I would feel the urge to explain to them in an elusive manner the fate that awaits them if they open up too much. I don't want to be responsible for someone being shipped out and banged up on an island.

Then there's the possibility I could be back here myself if I don't play ball. I want to sleep at night. I don't want to do this anymore. Going down this route was a big mistake.

The only thing I could think about at the time when I signed up for this was getting back home to carry on with my own routine, and now this could be a 24/7 'albatross around my neck'. What have I done? More to the point, what do I do?

Tomorrow is, I guess, 'graduation day' of sorts. Everyone's looking forward to going home and doing what they've been trained to do, except for me and Michael. Just as I thought, he's decided he wants to remain here of his own freewill, happy with his lot. Kinda makes me envious of his simple accepting ways. He'll be shuttling new arrivals to and fro every day, not a care in the world; ignorance can be bliss, I guess.

Graduation day, the day has come. It's kinda strange. After tomorrow, no dormitory. People I've grown accustomed to living with over the last three months I'll see no more. All the ups and downs, the people who've left to go who knows where. We were all expecting some kind of ceremony, some roll call, achievements announced, applause, and then handed a certificate. But no such party, just the revered hat handed to us and a manual of dos and don'ts, can-dos and cannots, and a footnote on the consequences of not doing the job by the book, a cold goodbye, but freedom awaits. This is it, it's all over at last.

I pinch myself, and yes, it is. Let's get the hell out of here. We stand and wait in line with our meagre belongings, ready for the bus to take us back to the dock, and we're greeted by a chirpy, cheerful, big red-faced Michael, who invites some twenty or so of us onboard, as if we're going on a trip to San Tropez or somewhere exciting. I gotta give this guy credit. His enthusiasm is boundless. The bus must be fifty years old. Off we go rattling down a potholed road to the sound of 'The Doors' on the radio playing 'This is the end, my beautiful friend, the end'. Very fitting.

We begin to gather speed. The idiot's got his pedal to the metal as we're approaching a bend. We're holding on with white knuckles to the metal bars across the bench seats in front, all shouting and screaming, "Slow the fuck down, slow down," only to fall on Michael's deaf ears. We spin out of control, hit the safety barrier, we're all out of our seats being shook up like beans in a tin can, and over we go to see only the sky and the ocean, as we barrel-roll into the air. This is it, this is the end, we're free-falling, going down.

A voice in my head is calling me, "Shane, Shane, wake up, where's your hat? Where's your hat?" and I'm shouting back, "I'm wearing my bloody hat, can't you see."

"You *are* funny," the voice replies, "you don't wear your hat in bed, silly. It's raining outside, you're going to need your hat."

I awake from the deepest sleep and the craziest dream I've ever had, to see my wife standing over me, smiling.

"Come on darling, you're going to be late for work," she says, "oh, and I've found your hat."

THE END

(For now)

Contact the author on:
shaunpayne1955@yahoo.com